HOPSCOTCH
TWISTY TALES

Cinderella's Big Foot

by Laura North
and Martin Remphry

W
FRANKLIN WATTS
LONDON•SYDNEY

This story is based on the traditional fairy tale,
Cinderella, but with a new twist.
You can read the original story in
Hopscotch Fairy Tales. Can you make
up your own twist for the story?

First published in 2010 by
Franklin Watts
338 Euston Road
London
NW1 3BH

Franklin Watts Australia
Level 17/207 Kent Street
Sydney
NSW 2000

Text © Laura North 2010
Illustrations © Martin Remphry 2010

A CIP catalogue record for this book is available
from the British Library.

ISBN 978 1 4451 0178 1 (hbk)
ISBN 978 1 4451 0184 2 (pbk)

Series Editor: Melanie Palmer
Series Advisor: Catherine Glavina
Series Designer: Peter Scoulding

Printed in China

Franklin Watts is a division of
Hachette Children's Books,
an Hachette UK company
www.hachette.co.uk

For Sue and Michael.
L.N.

Once upon a time, Cinderella lived
with her two ugly stepsisters.

They made her wear rags and clean the kitchen all day long.

"Scrub those pots!" said one sister.
"Clear up this mess," ordered
the other.

One day, a gold invitation
to the royal ball arrived.
"Cinderella, you will stay here and
clean while we meet the prince!"
laughed the ugly sisters.

"I wish I could go to the ball," sobbed Cinderella.

Suddenly, a woman with wings
appeared in a puff of smoke.
"I'm your fairy godmother!"

"Poor Cinderella, you will go to
the ball!" she said kindly.

She tapped her wand three times.
Cinderella's dirty rags became a
beautiful white dress. Her shoes
sparkled with diamonds.

Cinderella rushed off to the ball, without thanking her fairy godmother. She had one thing on her mind: the prince.

"The prince will fall in love with
me because I am so beautiful!"
boasted Cinderella.

All the girls wanted to meet the
prince. Cinderella pushed them
aside. "He's mine!" she yelled.

13

The handsome prince saw
Cinderella stamp on one girl's toes
and pull another girl's hair.

But the prince fell in love with her anyway. She didn't let anyone else near him! They danced together all night.

Then, as the clock struck midnight,
Cinderella's lovely white dress
turned back into dirty rags.

She ran away in shame. She was
in such a hurry that one of her
shoes fell off as she ran!

The next day, there was a loud knock at Cinderella's door. It was the prince!

"My true love lost her shoe," he declared. "I will marry the girl whose foot it fits."

"Get out of my way, ugly!" said Cinderella, pushing past her sisters. She moved her tiny foot towards the tiny shoe.

Suddenly, there was a BANG
and a big puff of smoke. The fairy
godmother was back!

"Cinderella!" she said, "you are just as mean as your sisters. You don't deserve to marry the prince!"

The fairy godmother tapped her magic wand three times. Cinderella's foot grew ...

and grew ...

and grew!

Now her foot was too big
for the shoe!

"You've got too big for your boots,"
laughed one sister.

"You've put your foot in it now!"
cackled the other.

"Oh fairy godmother, I know I've been bad," wept Cinderella. "If you shrink my foot back, I'll never be horrible again."

"Very well," the fairy godmother replied. "If you promise to be good, even to your stepsisters."

A week later, there was a royal wedding. Cinderella kept her word. She invited her stepsisters and even let them be her bridesmaids.

But *they* were just as rude
and horrible as before!

Puzzle 1

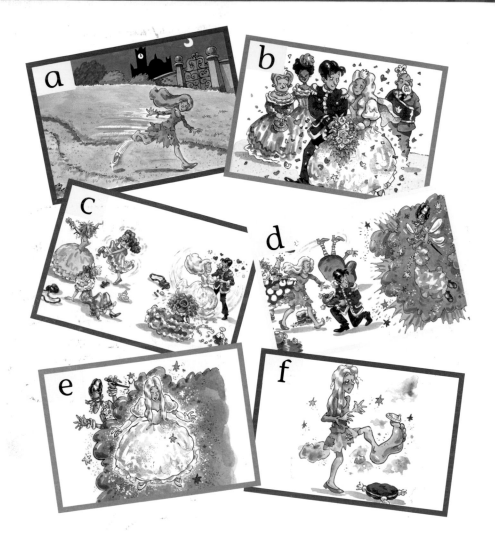

Put these pictures in the correct order.
Which event do you think is most important?
Now try writing the story in your own words!

Puzzle 2

Choose the correct speech bubbles for each character. Can you think of any others? Turn over to find the answers.

Answers

Puzzle 1

The correct order is: 1e, 2c, 3a, 4d, 5f, 6b

Puzzle 2

Cinderella: 2, 5

The prince: 1, 4

The fairy godmother: 3, 6

Look out for more Hopscotch Twisty Tales and Fairy Tales:

TWISTY TALES

The Three Little Pigs and the New Neighbour
ISBN 978 1 4451 0175 0*
ISBN 978 1 4451 0181 1

Jack and the Bean Pie
ISBN 978 1 4451 0176 7*
ISBN 978 1 4451 0182 8

Brownilocks and the Three Bowls of Cornflakes
ISBN 978 1 4451 0177 4*
ISBN 978 1 4451 0183 5

Cinderella's Big Foot
ISBN 978 1 4451 0178 1*
ISBN 978 1 4451 0184 2

Little Bad Riding Hood
ISBN 978 1 4451 0179 8*
ISBN 978 1 4451 0185 9

Sleeping Beauty – 100 Years Later
ISBN 978 1 4451 0180 4*
ISBN 978 1 4451 0186 6

FAIRY TALES

The Three Little Pigs
ISBN 978 0 7496 7905 7

Little Red Riding Hood
ISBN 978 0 7496 7901 9*
ISBN 978 0 7496 7907 1

Goldilocks and the Three Bears
ISBN 978 0 7496 7903 3

Hansel and Gretel
ISBN 978 0 7496 7904 0

Rapunzel
ISBN 978 0 7496 7900 2*
ISBN 978 0 7496 7906 4

Rumpelstiltskin
ISBN 978 0 7496 7902 6*
ISBN 978 0 7496 7908 8

The Elves and the Shoemaker
ISBN 978 0 7496 8543 0

The Ugly Duckling
ISBN 978 0 7496 8538 6*
ISBN 978 0 7496 8544 7

Sleeping Beauty
ISBN 978 0 7496 8545 4

The Frog Prince
ISBN 978 0 7496 8540 9*
ISBN 978 0 7496 8546 1

The Princess and the Pea
ISBN 978 0 7496 8541 6*
ISBN 978 0 7496 8547 8

Dick Whittington
ISBN 978 0 7496 8542 3*
ISBN 978 0 7496 8548 5

Cinderella
ISBN 978 0 7496 7417 5

Snow White and the Seven Dwarfs
ISBN 978 0 7496 7418 2

The Pied Piper of Hamelin
ISBN 978 0 7496 7419 9

Jack and the Beanstalk
ISBN 978 0 7496 7422 9

The Three Billy Goats Gruff
ISBN 978 0 7496 7420 5

The Emperor's New Clothes
ISBN 978 0 7496 7421 2